I0772393

ACKNOWLEDGMENT

Thank you to my daughter Sydney for giving me the nudge, and to Dave for illustrating this lovely story so long ago.

May this story bring you joy and happiness while you read it to a child who is adventurous enough to find friendship in many places.

ABOUT THE AUTHOR

Author Jenn L.S. Roberts has been friends with illustrator David Palluck since childhood, and like so many others never thought to pursue publishing a children's book. Jenn wrote this book many, many years ago, and it was illustrated at the same time, but is sat for years, with no one to read its lovely story.

Until a few years ago when her daughter, Sydney, urged her to publish itso everyone could enjoy the story of friendship. Friendship in some of the places we never think of. All we hope is you enjoy it as much as we do.

FRIENDSHIP IS EVERYWHERE

JONNY
AND
OTIS

ILLUSTRATED BY
DAVID PALLUCK

WRITTEN BY
JENN L.S. ROBERTS

Once upon a time on a green lush hill, stood a tiny oak tree with a big heart named Otis, who was very lonely.

This little tree had no one to come and sit beneath him, until one day a young boy by the name of Jonny, who was 8 or so, came with his big yellow truck and bright red fire engine, sat under Otis and started to play.

After that day Jonny came every day and played for hours upon hours with his trucks and little G.I Joe dolls. Jonny even made a fort in Otis and climbed to the very top of Otis to see the big blue sky.

Then one day when Jonny came to play he had no trucks or G.I Joes dolls, but a book, paper, and pencils. Jonny sat against Otis and began to study.

Otis did not understand why Jonny had no toys, he was confused, but Jonny was there with him, so it didn't matter what he brought with him, just as long as he was there.

Otis was very happy because he had someone to keep him company and sit beneath him. He had never had a friend, a real friend.

Then Otis noticed someone else with Jonny one day, a young girl. She was tall and very beautiful but Otis did not like her with his friend, he was very jealous.

I LOVE CHARLENE

Jonny cut into Otis with a big shinning knife and hurt him very badly. Jonny wrote, "I love Charlene," and he cut a heart around it and cut an arrow through the heart.

Otis winced in pain, shaking his branches and rustling his leaves, but Jonny was too overwhelmed with the sparkling eyes of Charlene to notice.

Otis cried and cried, because he did not understand why Jonny would want to hurt him, he was his friend.

After that awful day Jonny did not return to see Otis every day, until one strange day when the sky above was a shade of blue and not a single white cloud was to be seen.

Otis noticed Jonny, Charlene, and a young boy who was named Wyatt, about 8 or so.

Jonny showed Wyatt the cut heart in Otis and said, "This is not a thing to do to this nice tree, it hurts them, and when I was young I did not know any better, so don't hurt this nice tree, Okay?"

From then on Otis was never lonely again because Wyatt came and played with his toys and climbed Otis's limbs every day.

THE

END